# Sarah's Surprise

**Sally Hobart Alexander**

Illustrated by **Jill Kastner**

Macmillan Publishing Company   New York

Collier Macmillan Publishers   London

AUTHOR'S NOTE

Because mussels on the Pacific and North Atlantic coasts are not
always safe to eat, be sure to check with newspapers, radio stations,
and departments of marine resources before you go musseling.

Macmillan Publishing Company
866 Third Avenue, New York, NY 10022
Collier Macmillan Canada, Inc.
Printed and bound in Hong Kong
First American Edition

10 9 8 7 6 5 4 3 2 1

The text of this book is set in 15 point ITC Zapf International Medium.
The illustrations are rendered in oil on gessoed paper.

Library of Congress Cataloging-in-Publication Data
Alexander, Sally Hobart.    Sarah's surprise/Sally Hobart Alexander;
illustrated by Jill Kastner. —1st ed.    p.    cm.
Summary: Fearful Sarah comes to the rescue when her
mother hurts her ankle while hiking on the beach.
ISBN 0-02-700391-4
[1. Fear—Fiction.    2. Beaches—Fiction.]
I. Kastner, Jill, ill.    II. Title.
PZ7.A3779Sar   1990   [E]—dc20
89-36780   CIP   AC

To Kate and Bob Hobart
and Ruth and Fred Alexander

—S. H. A.

To my grandparents, who always
made me challenge myself

—J. K.

Sarah glanced out the window as Dad steered the car through the woods and down the short drive to the beach.

"What if the rocks are slippery?" Sarah asked.

"We'll walk slowly," Mom said, smiling back at her from the front seat.

"But what if the hike is too hard for me?"

"It won't be, not a strong seven-year-old like you."

Sarah wasn't so sure. When the car stopped, she got out slowly.

"I'll pick you ladies up in two hours," said Dad.

"We'll have a big surprise for you then," said Mom. "Won't we, Sarah?"

Sarah smiled, thinking about their secret.

But as she watched Dad drive off, her smile faded. "What if the mussels pinch me, like crabs do sometimes?"

"They don't have claws, honey. We had them for dinner last summer, remember?"

"Those mushy things? They made me sick!"

Mom grinned. "You never even tried one."

"That's 'cause it *would* have made me sick!"

"Well, Dad loves them. What better surprise for his birthday dinner."

From her backpack Mom pulled out a map. Sarah peeked while Mom studied it.

"Here we are at Singing Sands, Sarah. Shall we hike to Baldhead or Hermit Cliff?"

"Baldhead." Sarah laughed. "To remind us of Dad."

Mom winked. "Then let's rustle us some mussels!"

Sarah followed Mom and climbed easily on the rocks. Although they weren't very slippery, she was still worried. "What if I fall?"

"Just brush yourself off and keep going," said Mom. "Unless you're hurt. Then I'll help you."

Sarah passed wildflowers of every color—red and gold and orange. Her favorites were blue. "What are those flowers, Mom?"

"Lupines—strong, hardy flowers."

She saw them everywhere, even tucked into cliffs.

Sarah hiked along the ragged line of rock. Below her was the water, in some places a beach.

When she passed a few ducks, the sun dipped behind a cloud and the wind picked up. Sarah shivered.

"Better put this on," said Mom, handing Sarah a sweatshirt. Mom zipped up her jacket. "It was supposed to be beautiful today."

"What if it rains?" Sarah asked.

Mom tugged Sarah's ponytail. "Stop worrying. I'll take care of you."

After a few feet the path gave
way to jutting rocks, separated by
crevasses.

"What if I slip into one of those?"

"They aren't deep. Just take
your time."

"But how do I walk on them?"

"Sit like this, and stretch your foot
to the next rock."

Sarah tried, getting a toe, then her
whole foot on the next ledge.

"Good girl!" Mom showed her
what to do when the rock sloped up
again. "First reach with your hands,
then put your feet squarely
on the rock."

When they arrived at Baldhead, Sarah cried, "We're here! Yippee!" She held out her arms and felt the wind whip past them. Over her the sky looked like a big gray tent. She slid on her bottom beside Mom down the smooth rock to the V-shaped cove.

The water didn't cover all the tidepools yet, so Sarah stepped into the first one she found. "Yikes!" The icy water bit into her legs.

"Look through the water, honey. See those mussels on the rocks?"

"Those shiny, black things?"

"Yes," said Mom as she plucked one and held it up.

"It has a beard, like Dad." Sarah laughed and picked another.

"Good, Sarah. Take only the ones that are bigger than your thumb."

Sarah plopped the little shellfish into a string bag. "I still won't eat you, mushy mussels!"

"Maybe you'll change your mind," said Mom.

"Not me."

"Well, let's hurry, honey. I don't like this weather."

As if the sky heard, lightning flashed. And when they'd filled the bag, the rain came. No gentle drizzle; it poured.

"This way," said Mom. Sarah followed her up some low rocks to an opening carved by the waves. But the overhang gave little protection.

"I'll get some wood for a shelter," Mom called. "Stay there. No sense both of us getting soaked."

Sarah watched Mom gather wood and place it against the overhang. As lightning snapped and thunder boomed all around, Sarah bit her lip and tried to be brave.

But then she saw Mom fall. Sarah ran to her.

"Go back, honey. I'm all right."

Sarah took the wood and helped Mom to the shelter. Together they fixed the last board in place and ducked inside.

Mom took off her shoe and sock.

"It's getting swollen!" Sarah cried.

"I gave it a good twist, honey. I don't know how I'll walk back."

"What are we going to do?"

"Wait until Dad finds us," answered Mom.

"But that will take forever!"

"No, honey. He's a good tracker."

Sarah stared at Mom's foot. "It looks really sore!"

As the rain beat against the driftwood, Sarah wondered how to comfort Mom. "Sing your funny words to 'I Know an Old Lady,' Mom."

Mom sang, "I know an old lady who swallowed a queen, how obscene...."

Giggling, Sarah joined in. But when she saw Mom wince, she jumped up. "We can't keep waiting. Maybe..." she said slowly, "I should get Dad."

"No, Sarah, I can't let you do that."

"But why not?"

"The rocks are a bit slippery."

"I'll walk slowly, honest."

"No, it's too hard."

"Not for a strong seven-year-old like me!" Sarah began to smile.

"But what if you fall?"

"I'll brush myself off and keep going."

Suddenly Mom smiled back.

"Besides, Mom, the tide's coming in. What if Dad goes the wrong way and is late finding us?"

"The water will cover our shelter," Mom answered with a frown. "Will you really go slowly, Sarah?"

"I promise."

"And on your bottom over the crevasses?"

Sarah nodded. "Stop worrying. I'll take care of you." She kissed Mom and stepped out.

Rain hit her face gently. Scrambling up the rocks, Sarah turned her feet sideways and reached with her hands. Even though the thunder and lightning had stopped, it still looked stormy.

Sarah took a deep breath and moved on deliberately to the hard stretch of rocks. Dropping to her bottom, she reached forward with her foot, stood, and sat down, over and over again. When the rocks sloped up, she balanced on one ledge and stretched toward the higher one.

Once, her footing gave way and she slid into a crevasse. She fought back tears and reached up and over again. This time she cut her hand on a rock. Then she found a bare spot, gripped it, and drew herself up.

As she rested and tried to calm down, she saw some lupines. "Strong, hardy flowers," Sarah remembered, and picked one. She stuck it into her belt loop and took courage. She stood up, determined to go on.

Finally Sarah arrived at the smooth part of the trail and sped along. At the sight of the car, she called, "Dad! Dad!" and leaped to the beach. But the car was empty.

"Where are you?" she asked aloud and almost started to cry. Tracks led through the wet sand to the rocks at the opposite side of the beach. But Dad was nowhere to be seen.

Sarah beeped the car horn three times every few minutes.
Soon she saw Dad's orange slicker and raced to him.

"Mom hurt her ankle, and the tide's coming in! Hurry!"
She pulled Dad to the path.

"You came back by yourself, Sarah?"

"Yes, but hurry. Her ankle's all swollen!"

At the top of Baldhead, Sarah caught her breath and pointed down the other side to the shelter. She was surprised to see Mom outside, leaning on some driftwood.

"I did it!" Sarah called to her.

Mom smiled and waved the mussels.

"What's in that bag?" asked Dad, guiding her down to Mom.

"Our surprise—mussels!"

"Mussels? But last summer you wouldn't even touch them!"

Sarah grinned. "Well, this year I might even eat them!"